j523.3
G945m

DETROIT PUBLIC LIBRARY

W9-CXU-277

AR

JAN - - 2011

HU

Space

The Moon

Charlotte Guillain

Heinemann Library
Chicago, Illinois

©2009 Heinemann Library
a division of Capstone Global Library LLC
Chicago, Illinois
All rights reserved. No part of this publication may be reproduced or transmitted in any form or by any means, electronic or mechanical, including photocopying, recording, taping, or any information storage and retrieval system, without permission in writing from the publisher.

Editorial: Rebecca Rissman, Charlotte Guillain, and Siân Smith
Picture research: Tracy Cummins and Heather Mauldin
Designed by Joanna Hinton-Malivoire
Printed and bound by South China Printing Company Limited

13 12 11 10 09
10 9 8 7 6 5 4 3 2 1

ISBN-13: 978-1-4329-2746-2 (hc)
ISBN-13: 978-1-4329-2753-0 (pb)

Library of Congress Cataloging-in-Publication Data
Guillain, Charlotte.
  The moon / Charlotte Guillain.
     p. cm. -- (Space)
  Includes bibliographical references and index.
  ISBN 978-1-4329-2746-2 (hc) -- ISBN 978-1-4329-2753-0 (pb)
 1. Moon--Juvenile literature. 2. Satellites--Juvenile literature. I. Title.
  QB582.G85 2008
  523.3--dc22
                                2008049161

Acknowledgments
The author and publisher are grateful to the following for permission to reproduce copyright material:
Alamy pp.**5** (©ImageState), **20** (©Stocktrek Images, Inc.); Getty Images pp. **10** (©Joe Drivas), **11** (©Joel Sartore), **13** (©NASA/Stringer), **19** (©Science Faction/NASA), **22** (©NASA/Stringer), **23a** (©Alamy/ImageState), **23c** (©NASA/Stringer); NASA pp. **9** (©GRIN), **16** (©GRIN/David R. Scott), **17** (©GRIN), **18** (©GRIN/David Scott), **23b** (©GRIN); Photo Researchers Inc pp.**8** (©Science Source/NASA), **12** (©Detlev van Ravensway), **21** (©SPL); Photolibrary pp.**4** (©Dennis Lane), **6** (©Corbis); Shutterstock pp.**7** (©Oorka), **15** (©David Scheuber).

Front cover photograph reproduced with permission of NASA (©JPL/USGS). Back cover photograph reproduced with permission of NASA (©GRIN).

Every effort has been made to contact copyright holders of any material reproduced in this book. Any omissions will be rectified in subsequent printings if notice is given to the publisher.

Contents

Space

The Moon is in space.

Space is up above the sky.

The Moon

The Moon is a ball of rock.

The Moon is smaller than Earth.

There is no air on the Moon.

There are no living things on
the Moon.

The Moon does not make its
own light.

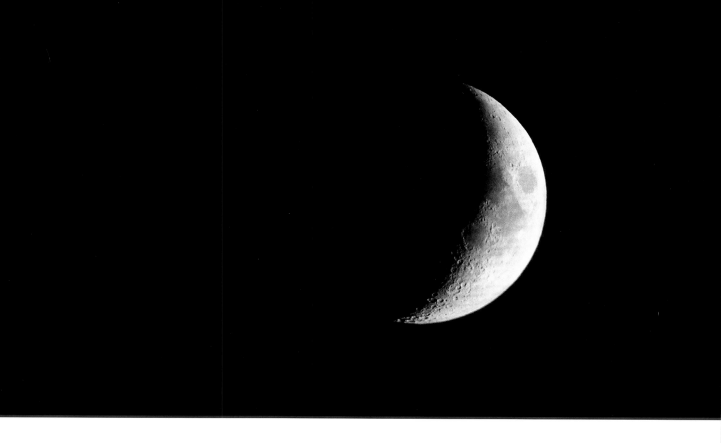

Light from the Sun makes the
Moon shine.

There is dust on the Moon.

crater

There are craters on the Moon.

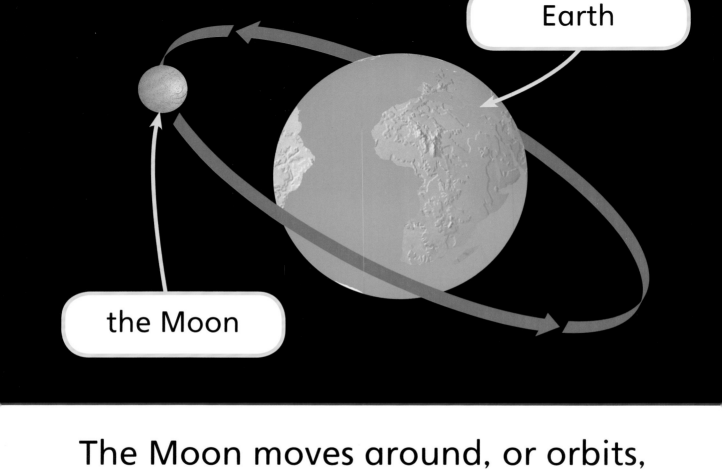

Earth

the Moon

The Moon moves around, or orbits, Earth.

We do not always see the whole
Moon as it orbits Earth.

Moon Landings

People have visited the Moon.

Astronauts landed on the Moon.

The astronauts collected rocks.

The astronauts looked around
the Moon.

Other Moons

There are other moons orbiting other planets.

Some planets have lots of moons.

Can You Remember?

What is this?

Answer on p. 24

Picture Glossary

 **air** gas we cannot see air that is all around us on Earth. We need to breathe in air to stay alive.

 **astronaut** person who travels into space

 **crater** hole in the ground, shaped like a bowl

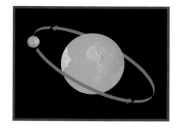 **orbit** move around

Index

Answer to question on p. 22: A crater.

Note to Parents and Teachers

Before reading

Ask children if they have seen the Moon. What shape was it? Did the Moon look the same every time they saw it? Have they ever seen the Moon during the day? Explain that the Moon goes around the Earth and that it is smaller than the Earth. The Moon does not make its own light. The light from the Sun makes the Moon shine.

After reading

• Make moon craters. Talk about the craters on the Moon. Explain that craters were made by large rocks crashing onto the surface of the Moon. Place wet plaster of Paris in a shallow dish. Invite the children to drop marbles of different sizes into the wet plaster. Let the plaster dry and talk about how the marbles made dents in the surface of the plaster just as the rocks made the craters in the surface of the Moon.